W9-AZE-000

That Sky, That Rain

That Sky, That Rain

by Carolyn Otto • *illustrations by* Megan Lloyd

THOMAS Y. CROWELL • NEW YORK

That Sky, That Rain
Text copyright © 1990 by Carolyn B. Otto
Illustrations copyright © 1990 by Megan Lloyd
All rights reserved. No part of this book may be used or reproduced in any manner whatsoever without written permission except in the case of brief quotations embodied in critical articles and reviews. Printed in the United States of America. For information address Thomas Y. Crowell Junior Books, 10 East 53rd Street, New York, N.Y. 10022.

Typography by Andrew Rhodes

1 2 3 4 5 6 7 8 9 10

First Edition

jE

Library of Congress Cataloging-in-Publication Data
Otto, Carolyn.
That sky, that rain / by Carolyn Otto ; illustrations by Megan Lloyd.
p. cm.
Summary: As a rainstorm approaches, a young girl and her grandfather take the farm animals into the shelter of the barn and then watch the rain begin.
ISBN 0-690-04763-0 : $. — ISBN 0-690-04765-7 (lib. bdg.) : $
[1. Rain and rainfall—Fiction. 2. Farm life—Fiction.]
I. Lloyd, Megan, ill. II. Title.
PZ7.08794Th 1990 89-36582
[E]—dc20 CIP
AC

To Megan, and to my grandparents, Otto and Nicholson, with deep down love.

—CBO

To Carolyn, of course, and to Tom, who saw the rain when there was none.

—MLL

The artist wishes to thank Pete Kutulakis; Cary D'Alo Place; and Dorothy Israel of Birdsong Gordon Setters.

Look at that sky.
We're in for some weather now.

Let's go, Sullivan. Lazybones.
It's going to pour any minute.

I always wanted a beard like that,
like old wire, wire and white paste.
Wouldn't your grandma just die?

GAS

Hold out your hands—both hands.
Whoa now. Talk soft now.
See there how her ears come up?

What a racket! What a fuss!
Sullivan, who asked you to sing?

This year I named them after my dinner—
Sweet Corn, Ambrosia, Okra, and Stew.
Stew? says your grandma. Ambrosia!
Next time, she says, I name the pigs.

Come on, Bessie. Come on now.
No sense waiting around for the rain.
Bessie and Bossie, Bossie and Bessie,
those are good names for cows.

Here she comes.

Stand here in the doorway and watch
how rain marks the edges of things—

the overhang of that white awning,

the space beneath the truck.

It's the most commonplace kind of magic,
clouds spilling down before your eyes.

You can open your mouth and drink
sky like a tall glass of water.

Look at that rain!